Checkerboard Animal Library Dogs

Greater Swiss Mountain Dogs

Paige V. Polinsky

Checkerboard Library
An Imprint of Abdo Publishing
abdopublishing.com

McLEAN MERCER REGIONAL LIBRARY
BOX 505
RIVERDALE, ND 58565

abdopublishing.com

Published by Abdo Publishing, a division of ABDO, PO Box 398166, Minneapolis, MN 55439. Copyright © 2017 by Abdo Consulting Group, Inc. International copyrights reserved in all countries. No part of this book may be reproduced in any form without written permission from the publisher. Checkerboard Library™ is a trademark and logo of Abdo Publishing.

Printed in the United States of America, North Mankato, Minnesota.
062016
092016

THIS BOOK CONTAINS RECYCLED MATERIALS

Cover Photo: Shutterstock
Interior Photos: AP Images, p. 7; iStockphoto, p. 15; Shutterstock, pp. 1, 5, 9, 11, 13, 17, 19, 21

Series Coordinator: Tamara L. Britton
Editor: Liz Salzmann
Production: Mighty Media, Inc.

Library of Congress Cataloging-in-Publication Data

Names: Polinsky, Paige V., author.
Title: Greater Swiss mountain dogs / Paige V. Polinsky.
Description: Minneapolis, MN : Abdo Publishing, a division of ABDO, [2017] | Series: Dogs set 13 | Includes index.
Identifiers: LCCN 2016007744 (print) | LCCN 2016012842 (ebook) | ISBN 9781680781779 (print) | ISBN 9781680775624 (ebook)
Subjects: LCSH: Greater Swiss mountain dog--Juvenile literature.
Classification: LCC SF429.G78 P65 2016 (print) | LCC SF429.G78 (ebook) | DDC 636.73--dc23
LC record available at http://lccn.loc.gov/2016007744

Contents

The Dog Family 4

Greater Swiss Mountain Dogs 6

What They're Like 8

Coat and Color 10

Size 12

Care 14

Feeding 16

Things They Need 18

Puppies 20

Glossary 22

Websites 23

Index 24

The Dog Family

Dogs and humans have been friends for thousands of years. There have been many benefits of this long friendship! The first **domesticated** dogs warned humans of nearby predators. They also guarded livestock and helped people hunt. In return, humans gave the dogs food and a place by the fire.

Dogs were **bred** for different uses. They now come in many colors, shapes, and sizes. But they all belong to the family **Canidae**. Foxes, wolves, and coyotes also belong to this family. In fact, scientists believe the modern dog **evolved** from the gray wolf.

Today there are about 400 dog breeds worldwide. Some have special jobs, such as helping with **therapy**, rescue, or farming. Others are simply affectionate family dogs. But the greater Swiss mountain dog, or Swissy, does it all.

The greater Swiss mountain dog is a great pet and a hard worker.

Greater Swiss Mountain Dogs

The Swissy is a lover, but its ancestors were fighters! About 2,000 years ago, Julius Caesar's army crossed the Alps to invade **Gaul**. The soldiers in his army brought trained mastiffs with them. Over time, these war dogs were **bred** into four new mountain dog breeds. The Swissy is the oldest and largest of them.

Swiss farmers relied on the Swissy for many tasks. This hardworking breed even earned the nickname "the poor man's horse"! Swissies herded sheep and pulled carts of milk and cheese into town. They also guarded property and watched over children. And they were loyal, loving companions.

But these devoted dogs almost disappeared in the late 1800s. Farmers began purchasing machines for

Today, many Swissies pull carts in competitions.

farm jobs instead of **breeding** Swissies to do the work. Luckily, a group of breeders brought the Swissy back.

In 1968, the breed was introduced to the United States. The **American Kennel Club (AKC)** recognized the Swissy in 1995.

What They're Like

The affectionate Swissy is truly a gentle giant. It is calm, friendly, and social. Some call it a "**Velcro** dog" because it sticks so close to its family! This **breed** loves playing as much as it loves to work. And its patience makes it great with children.

But don't let a Swissy's sweet nature fool you. This **confident** canine is a natural guard dog. The Swissy is devoted to the safety of its home. It is wary of strangers and always on the alert. You'll hear its loud, deep bark whenever someone comes to the door!

This breed takes time to mature. As a puppy, it is mouthy and mischievous. As an adult, it can accidentally knock children over! But positive training will help the Swissy become a beloved family member.

This majestic breed is very dedicated to its family.

Coat and Color

The Swissy has a **dense** double coat. This kept it warm in the frosty Swiss mountains! But unlike many fluffy northern **breeds**, the Swissy's fur is short. Its topcoat is smooth, straight, and easy to clean. The Swissy fully **sheds** its heavy undercoat twice a year. Otherwise, it sheds lightly throughout the year.

The official breed standard is a black, white, and red coat. The topcoat is black with rust markings above the eyes. There are also rust markings on the cheeks and legs. The standard Swissy has white on its neck, chest, paws, and tail tip. There is also a blaze of white on its head.

Not all Swissies follow the breed standard, however. Some are blue, white, and tan. Others are red and white.

A thick double coat protects the Swissy from cold and snow.

Size

The Swissy is not called a "gentle giant" for nothing. This muscular, big-boned **breed** is very powerful. Fully grown males weigh between 105 and 140 pounds (48 and 64 kg). They stand 26 to 29 inches (66 to 74 cm) tall.

Female Swissies are smaller. They usually weigh between 85 and 110 pounds (39 and 50 kg). They stand 24 to 27 inches (61 to 69 cm) tall.

The noble Swissy is built for hard labor. It has a wide, deep chest and strong shoulders. Its thighs are broad and muscular. These features make the Swissy a skillful cart puller. It also has a long, straight tail.

This breed's skull is broad and flat. Its triangular, high-set ears hang close to its head. Its brown eyes are almond shaped. The Swissy is a "dry-mouth" breed. It doesn't tend to drool as much as some other breeds.

The Swissy is surprisingly swift for its huge size.

Care

Your Swissy will need basic grooming to look its best. Brush its fur weekly to reduce **shedding**. Trim its nails every month. And brush its teeth frequently. But be sure to use dog-friendly toothpaste!

The Swissy is usually a hardy dog. But it is also at risk for certain medical issues. **Bloat** and **incontinence** are common in the **breed**. And some Swissies experience "lick fits" caused by an upset stomach. During these fits, they will lick and eat anything within reach!

Schedule your Swissy for regular checkups with your veterinarian. The vet can check your pup for health issues and **spay** or **neuter** it. The vet can also **vaccinate** your Swissy. And you can avoid expensive vet bills by keeping small things out of reach. Swissies have been known to eat socks!

Weekly grooming will help your Swissy look and feel great.

Feeding

A balanced diet with moderate levels of fat and protein is key for a fit Swissy. And there are many dry, wet, and semi-moist foods to choose from! Start your Swissy out with the same food its **breeder** used.

The amount you feed your Swissy depends on certain factors. The dog's age, size, and lifestyle will determine its **nutritional** needs. Talk to your vet to decide what's best for your Swissy. And make any food changes gradually to help your pup adjust.

Be aware that your Swissy can **bloat** easily. Give it several small meals each day. Watch it closely, and don't let it eat too fast. If bloat does occur, bring your dog to the vet right away.

Your Swissy should always have fresh water to drink. But treats should be given in moderation.

Swissies that overeat are in danger of becoming **obese**. This can lead to heart disease, **diabetes**, and more. But a healthy diet will help your Swissy live a long, full life!

An active Swissy needs quality food to fuel its adventures.

Things They Need

A busy Swissy is a happy Swissy. This working dog needs low-key daily exercise. But the Swissy is no running companion. It can overheat easily because of its size and heavy coat. Hiking, playing, and weight pulling can help keep your pup active.

You will need a leash, collar, and identification tags for your dog. A comfortable crate will give it a place to rest when you're away. It will also help with **housebreaking**. Swissy pups are especially mouthy. So sturdy food dishes and chew toys are a must!

Your Swissy needs love and attention most of all. It is important for this large **breed** to be well behaved. Prepare to be a firm, patient leader. Early training and **socialization** are also important for a polite Swissy.

A Swissy can make a chew toy out of anything!

Puppies

A mother Swissy is **pregnant** for about 63 days. She gives birth to a **litter** of eight to ten puppies. These Swissy pups cannot see or hear. Their eyes and ears begin to work after two weeks. And after eight weeks, they can go to their new homes!

Take some time to pick the right Swissy for you. Choose a respectable **breeder** or animal shelter. When you find a puppy, get to know its personality. Ask questions about its health and parents.

It is never too early to train your Swissy. Start introducing it to new people and places right away. Use treats, praise, and play to reward good behavior. This breed takes longer to **housebreak** than most. So you will need to be patient!

New experiences will shape your Swissy pup into a happy, confident adult.

The work you put into training will pay off. Well-trained Swissies are easygoing and reliable. With love and care, your gentle giant will be a loving family member for 10 to 12 years.

Glossary

American Kennel Club (AKC) - an organization that studies and promotes interest in purebred dogs.

bloat - a condition in which food and gas trapped in a dog's stomach cause pain, shock, and even death.

breed - a group of animals sharing the same ancestors and appearance. A breeder is a person who raises animals. Raising animals is often called breeding them.

Canidae (KAN-uh-dee) - the scientific Latin name for the dog family. Members of this family are called canids. They include wolves, jackals, foxes, coyotes, and domestic dogs.

confident - having faith in oneself and one's powers.

dense - thick or compact.

diabetes - a disease in which the body cannot properly absorb normal amounts of sugar and starch.

domesticated - adapted to life with humans.

evolve - to develop gradually.

Gaul - an ancient European country that is now France and parts of Belgium, Germany, and Italy.

housebreak - to teach a dog to not go to the bathroom inside.

incontinence - the inability to control the release of urine from the body.

litter - all of the puppies born at one time to a mother dog.
neuter (NOO-tuhr) - to remove a male animal's reproductive glands.
nutritional - that which promotes growth, provides energy, repairs body tissues, and maintains life.
obese - having too much body fat.
pregnant - having one or more babies growing within the body.
shed - to cast off hair, feathers, skin, or other coverings or parts by a natural process.
socialization - adapting an animal to behaving properly around people or other animals in various settings.
spay - to remove a female animal's reproductive organs.
therapy - relating to the treatment of diseases and disorders.
vaccinate - to give someone a shot given to prevent illness or disease.
Velcro - the brand name of a type of fabric that has two sides that stick together.

Websites

To learn more about Dogs, visit **booklinks.abdopublishing.com**. These links are routinely monitored and updated to provide the most current information available.

Index

A
Alps 6, 10
American Kennel Club 7

B
barking 8
bloat 14, 16
body 10, 12, 14, 16
breeder 7, 16, 20

C
Caesar, Julius 6
Canidae (family) 4
character 4, 6, 8, 12, 18, 20, 21
chest 10, 12
coat 10, 14, 18
collar 18
color 10, 12
crate 18

E
ears 12, 20
exercise 18
eyes 10, 12, 20

F
food 16, 17, 18, 20

G
Gaul 6
grooming 14
guarding 4, 6, 8

H
head 10, 12
health 14, 16, 17, 18, 20
herding 6
history 4, 6, 7, 10
housebreaking 18, 20
hunting 4

L
leash 18
legs 10, 12
life span 17, 21
litter 20

N
nails 14
neck 10
neuter 14

P
paws 10
puppies 8, 20, 21

R
reproduction 20

S
senses 20
shedding 10, 14
size 6, 12, 16, 18
socialization 18
spay 14

T
tail 10, 12
teeth 14
training 8, 18, 20, 21

U
United States 7

V
vaccines 14
veterinarian 14, 16

W
war 6
water 16
working 4, 6, 8, 18